Baldwinsville Public Library
WITHDRAWN
JUN 2 0 2005
P9-DZX-886
DEPARTMENT
ENDS
SUPERHEATER
EXHAUST
Boiler
QUALITY

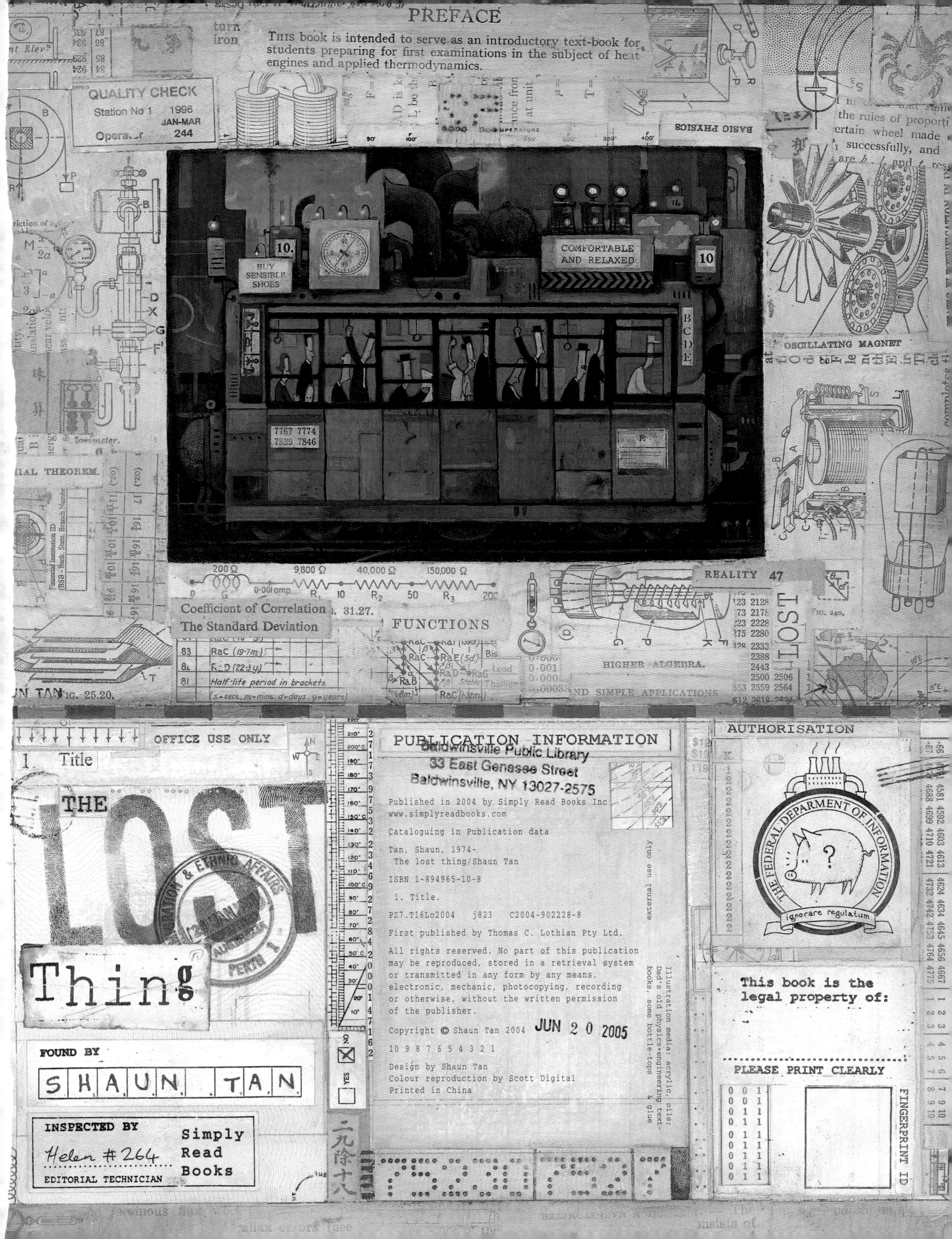

PUBLICATION INFORMATION

Published in 2004 by Simply Read Books Inc
www.simplyreadbooks.com

Cataloguing in Publication data

Tan, Shaun, 1974-
The lost thing/Shaun Tan

ISBN 1-894965-10-8

1. Title.

PZ7.T16Lo2004 j823 C2004-902228-8

First published by Thomas C. Lothian Pty Ltd.

10 9 8 7 6 5 4 3 2 1

Design by Shaun Tan
Colour reproduction by Scott Digital
Printed in China

Illustration media: acrylic, oils; Dad's old physics+engineering text-books, some bottle-tops & glue

external use only

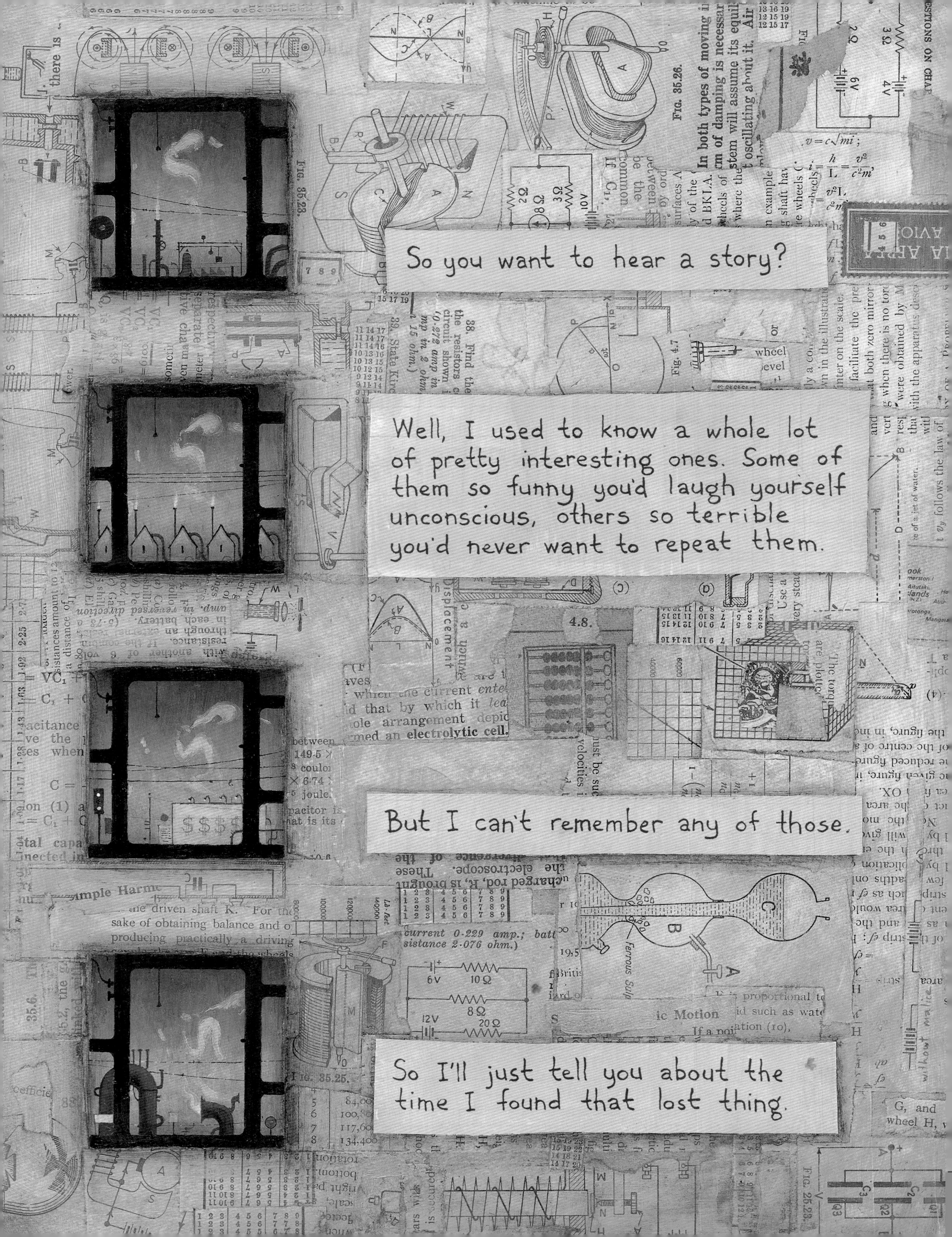

So you want to hear a story?
Well, I used to know a whole lot of pretty interesting ones. Some of them so funny you'd laugh yourself unconscious, others so terrible you'd never want to repeat them.
But I can't remember any of those.
So I'll just tell you about the time I found that lost thing.

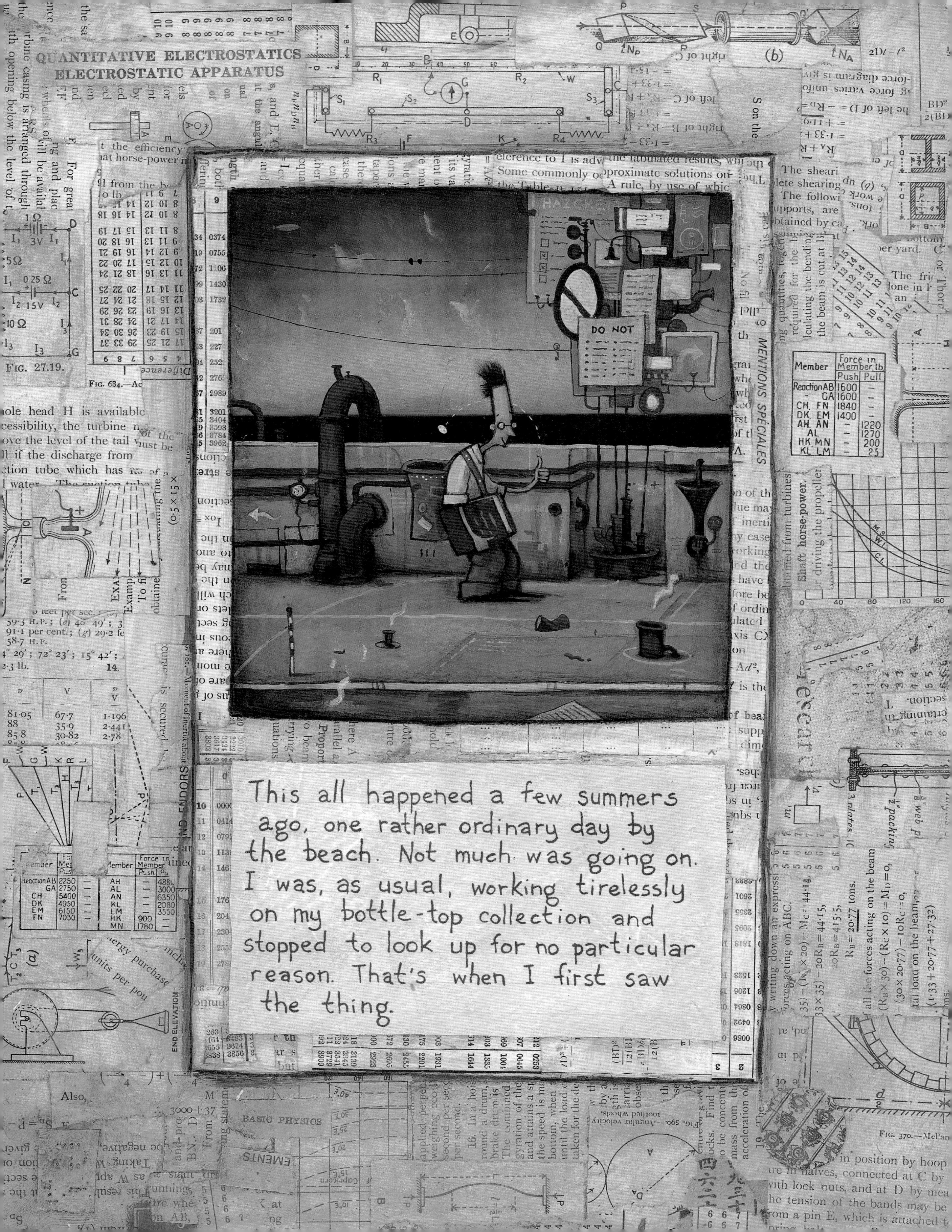
This all happened a few summers ago, one rather ordinary day by the beach. Not much was going on. I was, as usual, working tirelessly on my bottle-top collection and stopped to look up for no particular reason. That's when I first saw the thing.
DO NOT

I must have stared at it for a while. I mean, it had a really weird look about it — a sad, lost sort of look. Nobody else seemed to notice it was there. Too busy doing beach stuff, I guess.
BOIL
2·15
ELECTRICITY
NOTES
WHAT BOTTLE TOP IS THAT?
MORE

Naturally, I was intrigued. I decided to investigate.
FUEL
HOMOGENEOUS EQUATIONS
sure didn't do much.
It just sat there,
looking out of place.
I was baffled.

It was quite friendly though, once I started talking to it.

I played with the thing for most of the afternoon. It was great fun, yet I couldn't help feeling that something wasn't quite right.
As the hours slouched by, it seemed less and less likely that anybody was coming to take the thing home. There was no denying the unhappy truth of the situation It was lost.

I asked a few people if they knew anything about it, but nobody was very helpful.

ENTROPY AND SIMPLE APPLICATIONS
RECIPROCALS
Subtract Differences
What's in a Name?
YOU ARE HERE
Per cent. by Volume
21·8
8·7
69·5
AB
PERMUTATIONS AND COMBINATIONS.
Force in Member lb
Push Pull
TRIGONOMETRICAL FUNCTIONS
35.14. The Principle of the Alternator.—The
alternator is a machine for converting
into electrical energy and its principle

I took the lost thing over to Pete's place. Pete has an opinion on just about everything.

'Cool,' he said.

'I'm trying to find out who owns it,' I told him.
'I dunno, man,' said Pete. 'It's pretty weird. Maybe it doesn't belong to anyone. Maybe it doesn't come from anywhere. Some things are like that...' He paused for dramatic effect, '...just plain lost.'

underside of the piston
as, in this position, a through
assage to exhaust which may
INDETERMINATE EQUATIONS OF THE FIRST DEGREE.
ratchet wheel.
ELEMENTARY THERMODYNAMICS
Mg
2 Scope 18
3 Seeing Things 28
4 Reality 43
a metal anode, often called the
g the cathode and its function
electrons emitted by the latter.
ate, surro
s to collect
The base of
ired to raise 1 lb. of dry

There was nothing left to do but take the thing home with me. I mean, I couldn't just leave it wandering the streets. Plus I felt kind of sorry for it.
KEEP OU

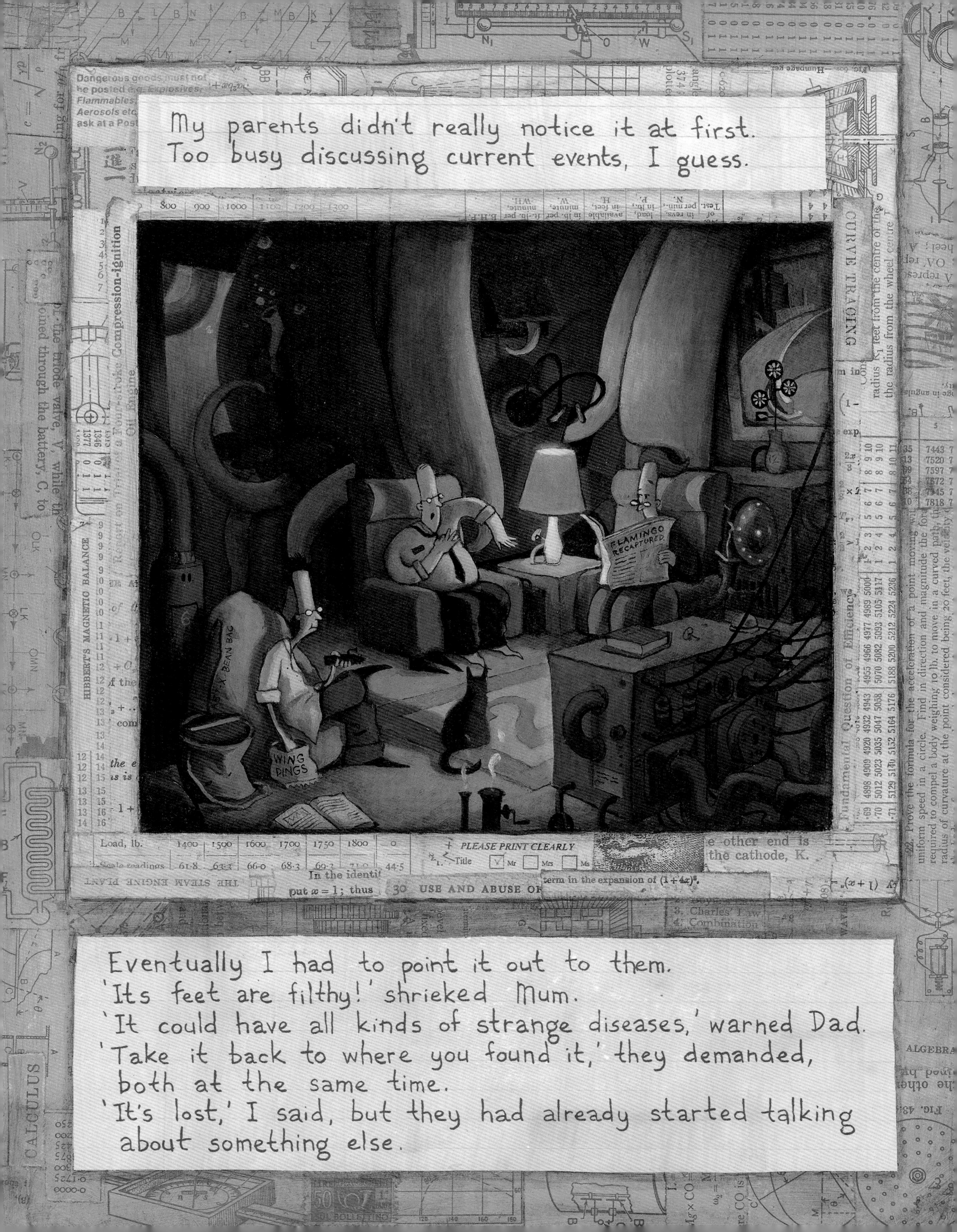
My parents didn't really notice it at first.
Too busy discussing current events, I guess.
FLAMINGO RECAPTURED
BEAN BAG
WING DINGS
Eventually I had to point it out to them.
'Its feet are filthy!' shrieked Mum.
'It could have all kinds of strange diseases,' warned Dad.
'Take it back to where you found it,' they demanded, both at the same time.
'It's lost,' I said, but they had already started talking about something else.

I hid the thing in our back shed and gave it something to eat, once I found out what it liked. It seemed a bit happier then, even though it was still lost.

I checked the local paper for any lost pet notices, but only found a lot of good deals on refrigerator repairs. I remember thinking then that Pete was probably right, that some things were just plain lost. In any case, I sure couldn't keep the thing in the shed forever. Mum or Dad would eventually notice it when they came out looking for a hammer or something.
It was a real dilemma.
I was wondering what to do when a small advertisement on the last page of the paper happened to catch my eye.

bureaucritae opacus.
Double sided for extra adhesion and durable enough to withstand the toughest bureaucratic exercises. No office desk is complete without a good spool of 20mm industrial-strength Red Tape.
ORDER NOW!!!
THE FEDERAL DEPARTMENT OF ECONOMICS
consumere ergo sum.
We understand that at the end of the da
all that matters is the balance sheet.
ODUCT RECALL
potentially lethal
ault has been identi-
ied in all model 350A
eluxe "Suck & Slice"
utomated beet-cutters
purchased before June
15, around 2:23pm.
Return for replacement
at your local Product
Recall Depot, with ap-
propriate appliance
receipt & registration
forms. The Federal De-
partment of Automated
Appliances apologises
for any inconvenience.
ARE YOU FINDING THAT THE ORDER OF DAY-TO-DAY LIFE IS UNEXPECTEDLY DISRUPTED BY
UNCLAIMED PROPERTY?
TROUBLESOME ARTIFACTS OF UNKNOWN ORIGIN?
OBJECTS WITHOUT NAMES?
THINGS THAT JUST DON'T BELONG?
FILING CABINET LEFTOVERS?
DON'T PANIC!
We've got a pigeon hole to stick it in.
THE FEDERAL DEPARTMENT OF ODDS & ENDS
sweepus underum carpetae.
Downtown,
6328th Street
Tall Grey Building #357b
DAY OR NIGHT
CALL OUT MOBILE
VISUAL TECHNICIANS
Instant, on-the-spot compositional solutions
* No location too obscure!
* No client too irritating!
* No plumbing too hard to draw!
A21/B
A21/C
ZX40
UXB42
DDU98
Zx(a)
TYX23
HU84-C
GL56
RF5(a)
ommunity Service Announcement
NOW YOUR DIODES
Can't seem to find a
C56/b transistorised
regulator with match-
ing field coil rotor
when you need one?
YOU'RE IN LUCK!
Quality Sprockets
SMITH & SMITH
& rotating parts
Flywheels, gears, sproc
wind-up things, fan belt
hard-to-find alternator
Look for the Giant Gyro
southbound expressway 54
Latest Twin Piston Exhaust Valves now available!
DEPARTMENT OF TUBES & PIPES
plumbiferus ductus.
HAVE you any perpetual-motion ideas? If so, send them in with a short explanation of how they are supposed to operate. For each one accepted and published, $5.00 will be paid. Selections will also be made from material which has been entered in this contest. A new Perpetual-
REMEMBER:
DON'T SIGN ANY AUTOMATED APPLIANCE CLEARANCE PERMIT UNTIL YOU'VE REGISTERED AN APPLICATION FOR HYDRAULIC TUBE FITTING IN ACCORDANCE WITH BYLAW 32b OF THE OFFICE OF MOTOR CALIBRATION'S SERVICE CODE.
And don't forget to fasten your wingnuts.

ALGEBRAIC EQUATIONS
VACUUM TUBES FOR ALL SEASONS
BOB'S GASKET EMPORIUM
The next morning we caught a tram into the city.
COMBUSTION CHAMBERS
HARMONICAL PROGRESSION.
FORCE ON CURRENT

combustion engi
essentials of a he
(i) The source o
(ii) The workin
after ignition of
behind the proje
FIG. 2.5—Steam nozzle.
DEAL DIRECT WITH
LABORATORIES
SAVE UP TO 50%
Laboratory and Experimental Work
ing and other applied sciences may be analysed
the main headings:—
wear so that the point
descends ultimately to E,
then EF is the axial wear,
and is constant for any point
on the bearing. EG is normal
80 ADVANCED 1936 FEATURES
CONSERVEZ
CE BILLET
is parallel to the tangent EH
at E. The normal wear is
EG, and may be assumed to
be proportional to the speed
of rubbing. The intensity of
MAIL COUPON TODAY!
FREE 30-DAY TRIAL OFFER and 40-
PAGE FOUR-COLOR FREE CATALOG

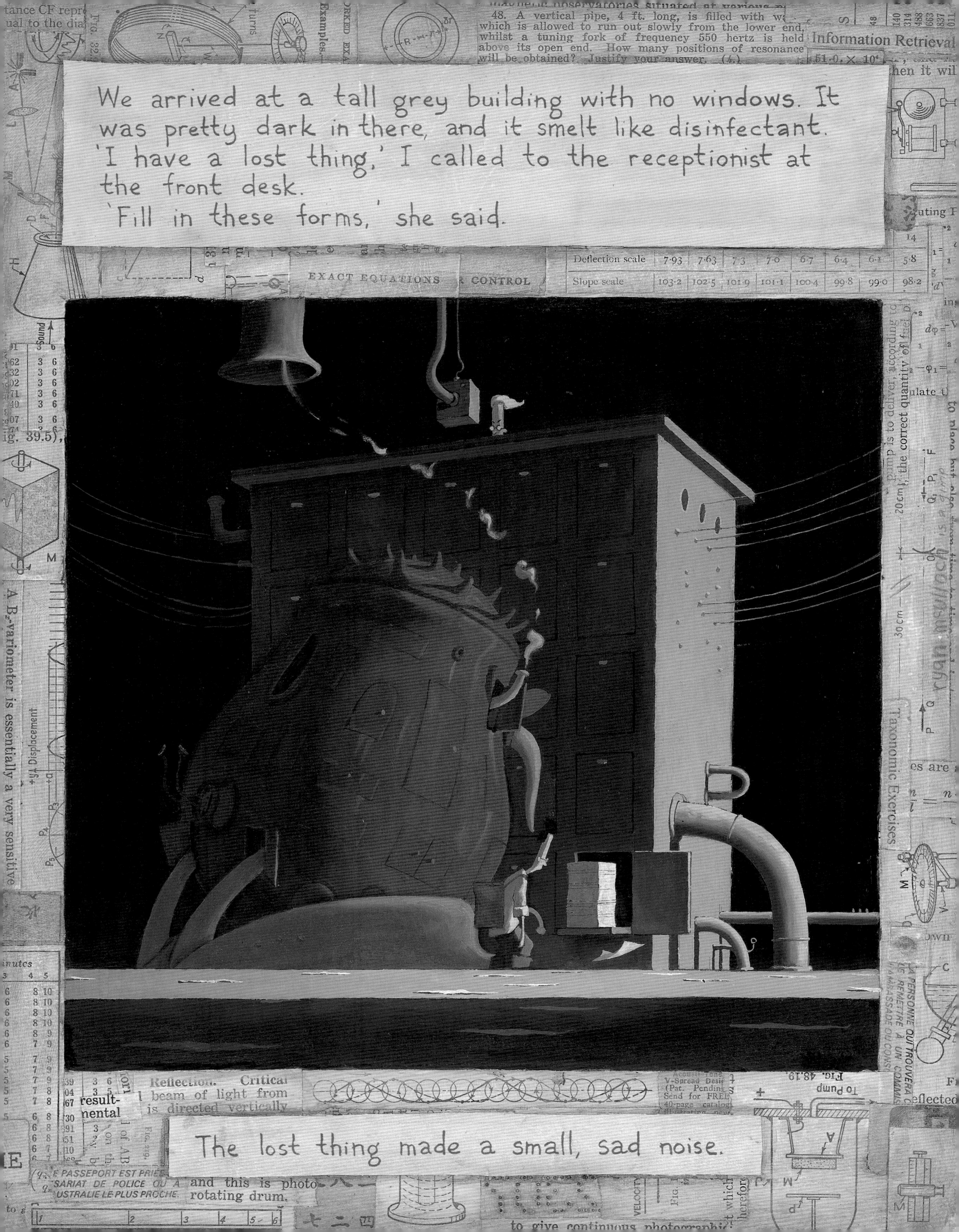
We arrived at a tall grey building with no windows. It was pretty dark in there, and it smelt like disinfectant.
'I have a lost thing,' I called to the receptionist at the front desk.
'Fill in these forms,' she said.
The lost thing made a small, sad noise.

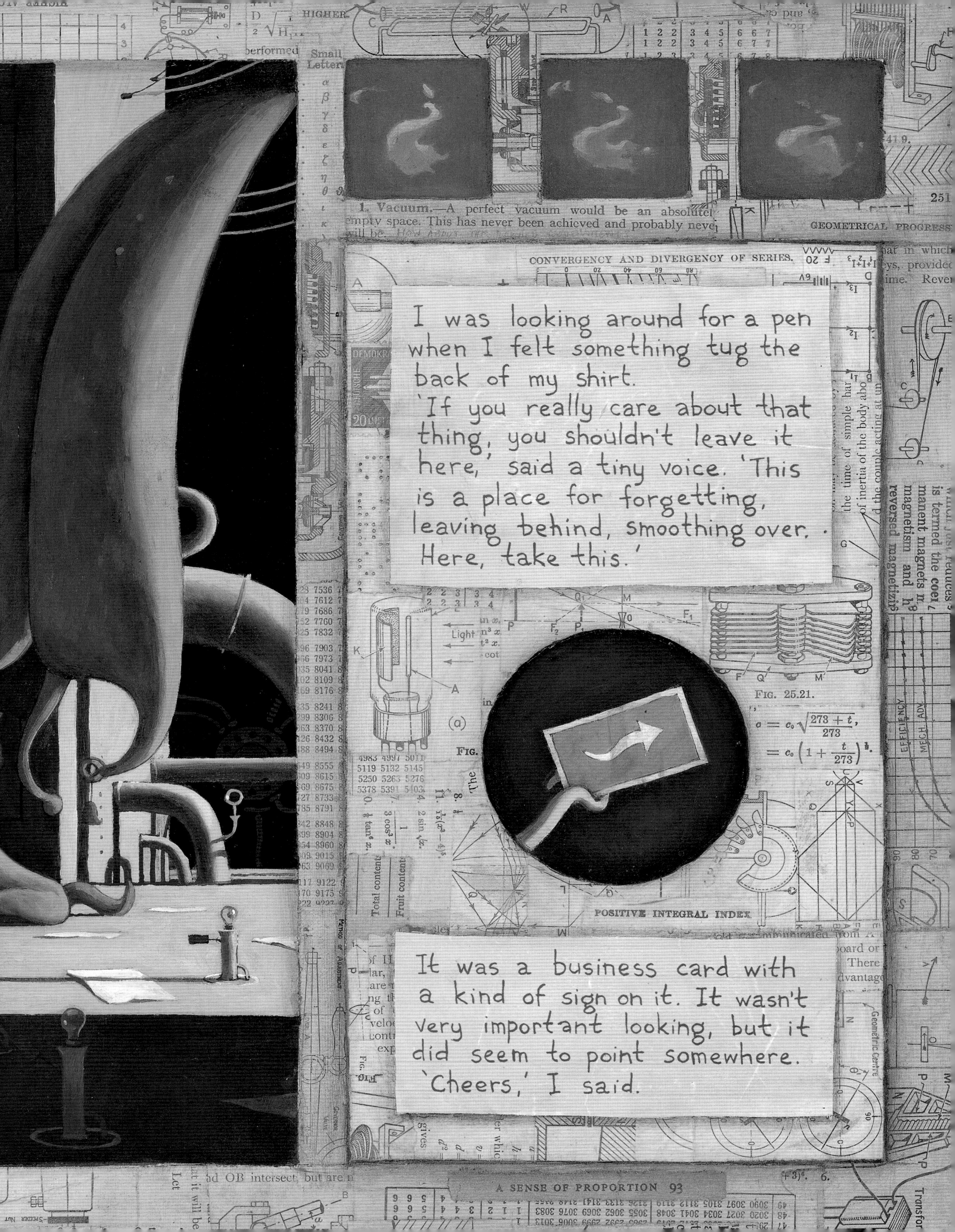
I was looking around for a pen when I felt something tug the back of my shirt.
'If you really care about that thing, you shouldn't leave it here,' said a tiny voice. 'This is a place for forgetting, leaving behind, smoothing over. Here, take this.'
It was a business card with a kind of sign on it. It wasn't very important looking, but it did seem to point somewhere.
'Cheers,' I said.

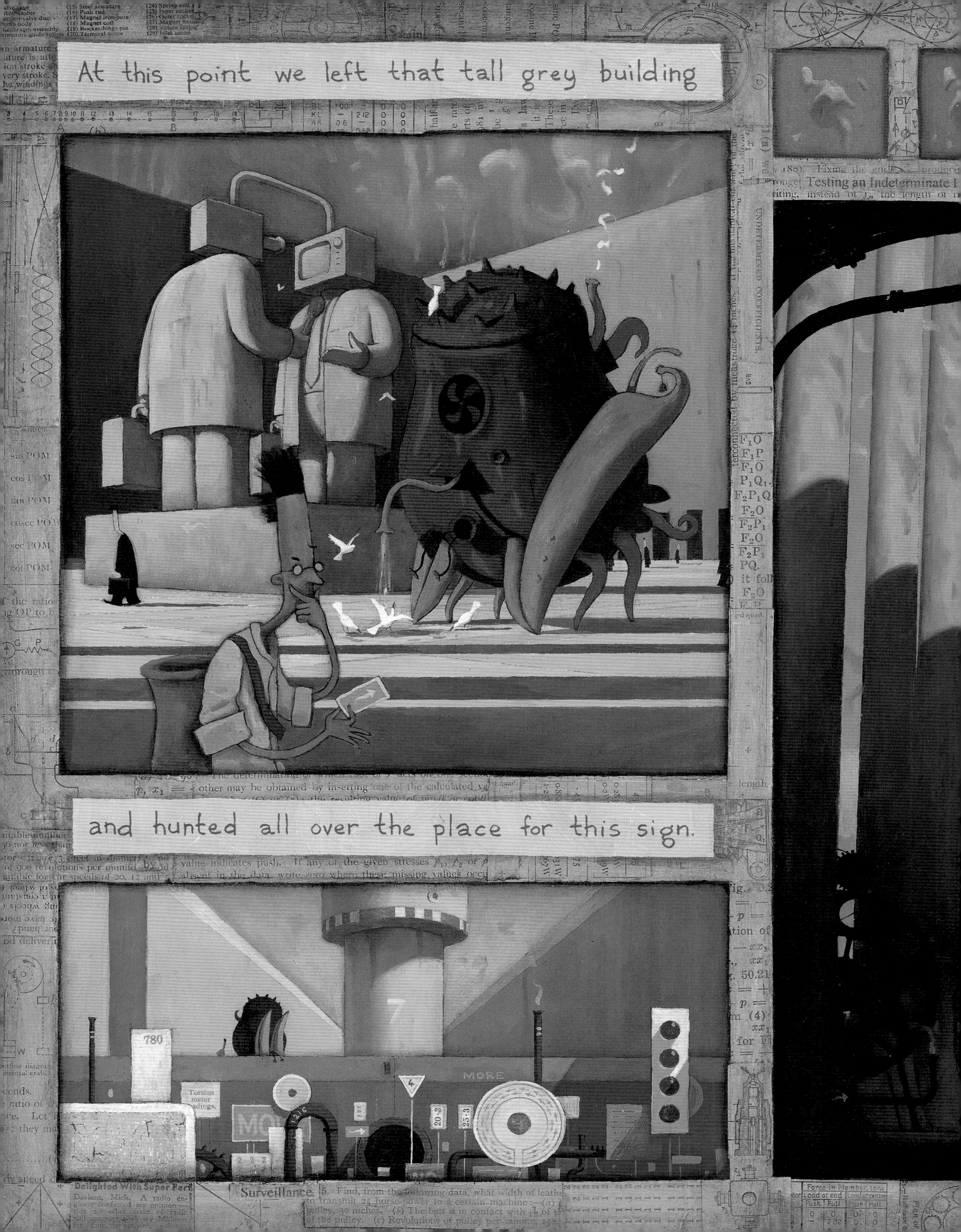
At this point we left that tall grey building
and hunted all over the place for this sign.
Testing an Indeterminate
780
MORE
Surveillance

It wasn't an easy job,
TODAY IS THE TOMORROW YOU WERE PROMISED YESTERDAY.
and I can't say I knew what it all meant.

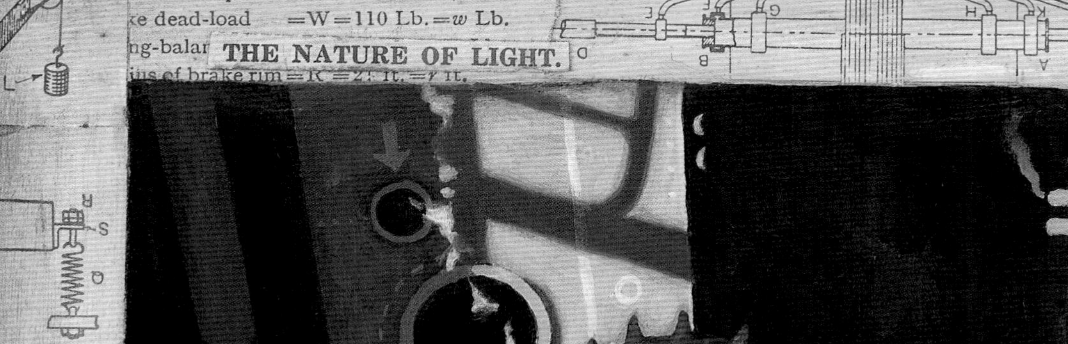
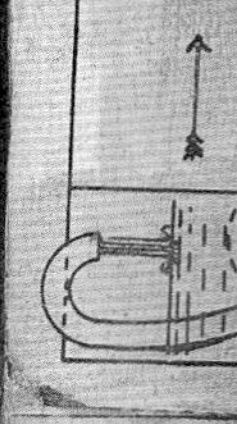
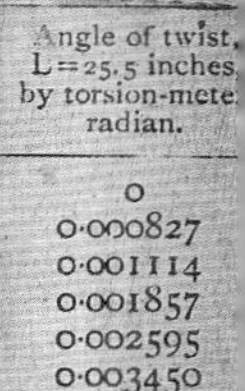

Eventually we found what seemed to be the right place, in a dark little gap off some anonymous little street. The sort of place you'd never know existed unless you were actually looking for it.
I pressed a buzzer on the wall and this big door opened up.

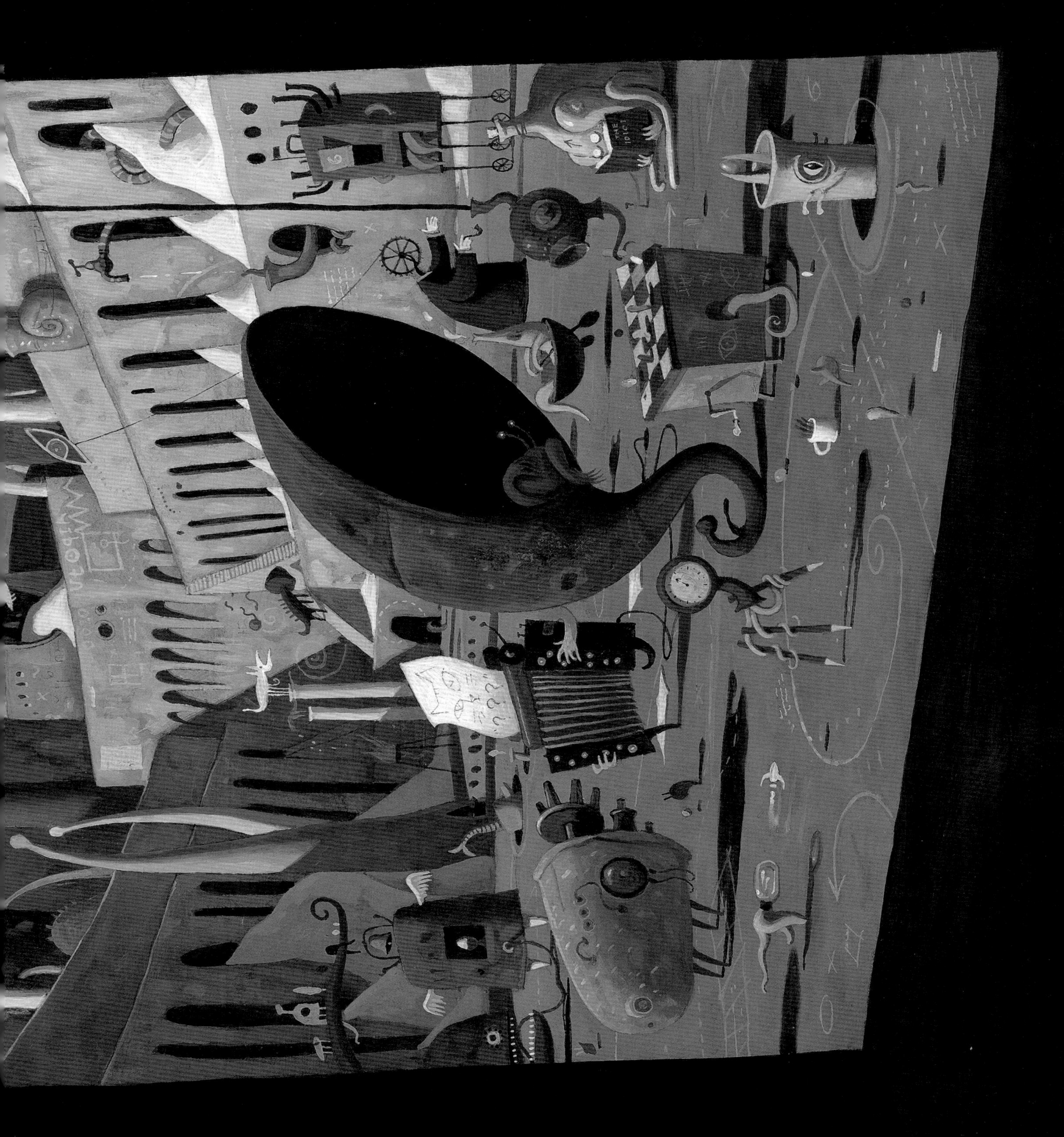

I didn't know what to think, but the lost thing made an approving sort of noise. It seemed as good a time as any to say goodbye to each other. So we did.
Heat Exchanger
Fig. 2.22—Closed circuit gas-turbine plant.
equal and opposite reactions
Electrical Insulation for FUN and PROFIT.
RECIPROCALS
Fig. 49.33.
VALID FOR ONE ENTRY ONLY.
Meaning
Then I went home to classify my bottle-top collection.
ADMIT
55002131 15

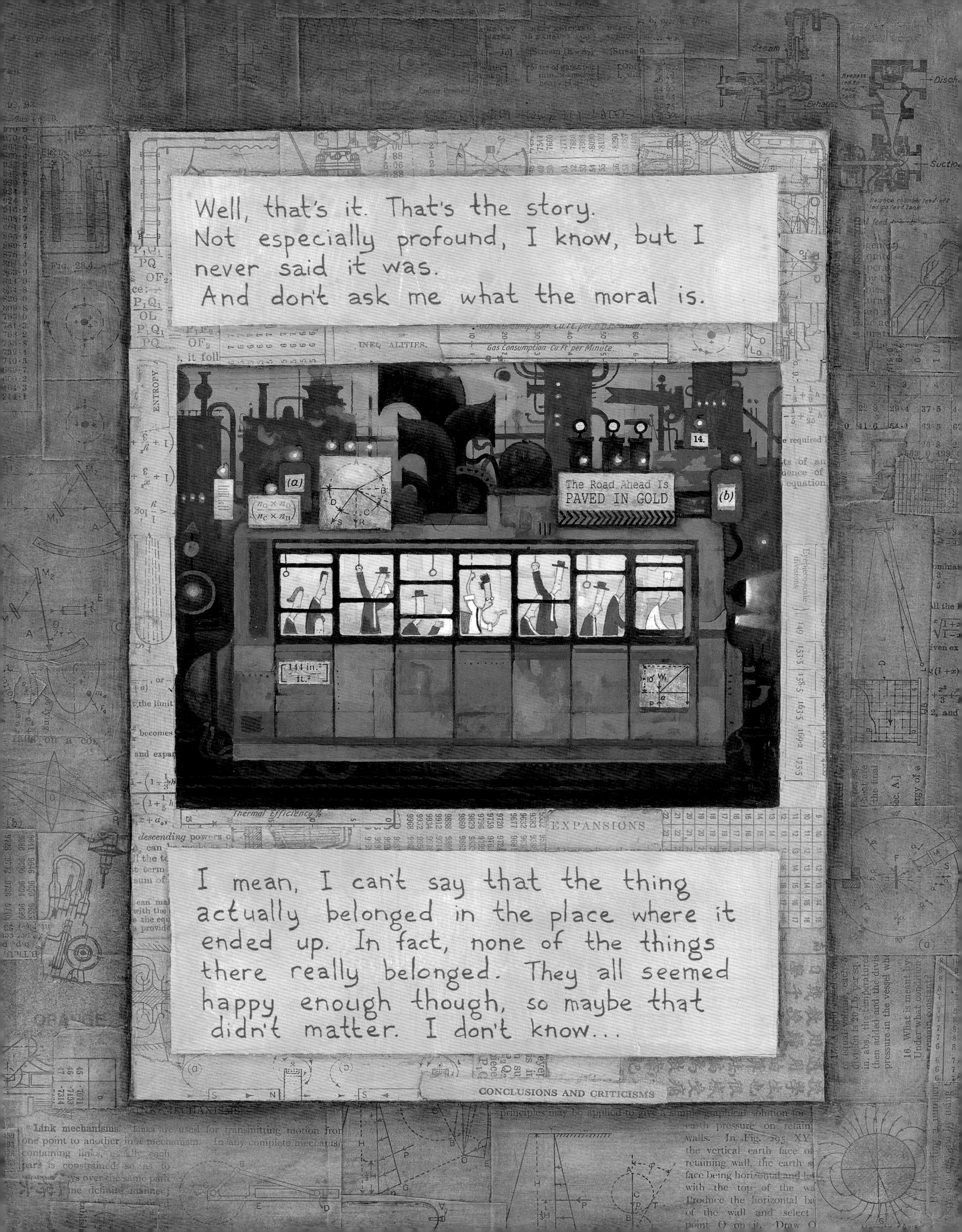
Well, that's it. That's the story.
Not especially profound, I know, but I never said it was.
And don't ask me what the moral is.
The Road Ahead Is
PAVED IN GOLD
I mean, I can't say that the thing actually belonged in the place where it ended up. In fact, none of the things there really belonged. They all seemed happy enough though, so maybe that didn't matter. I don't know...
CONCLUSIONS AND CRITICISMS

I still think about that lost thing from time to time. Especially when I see something out of the corner of my eye that doesn't quite fit.
You know, something with a weird, sad, lost sort of look.

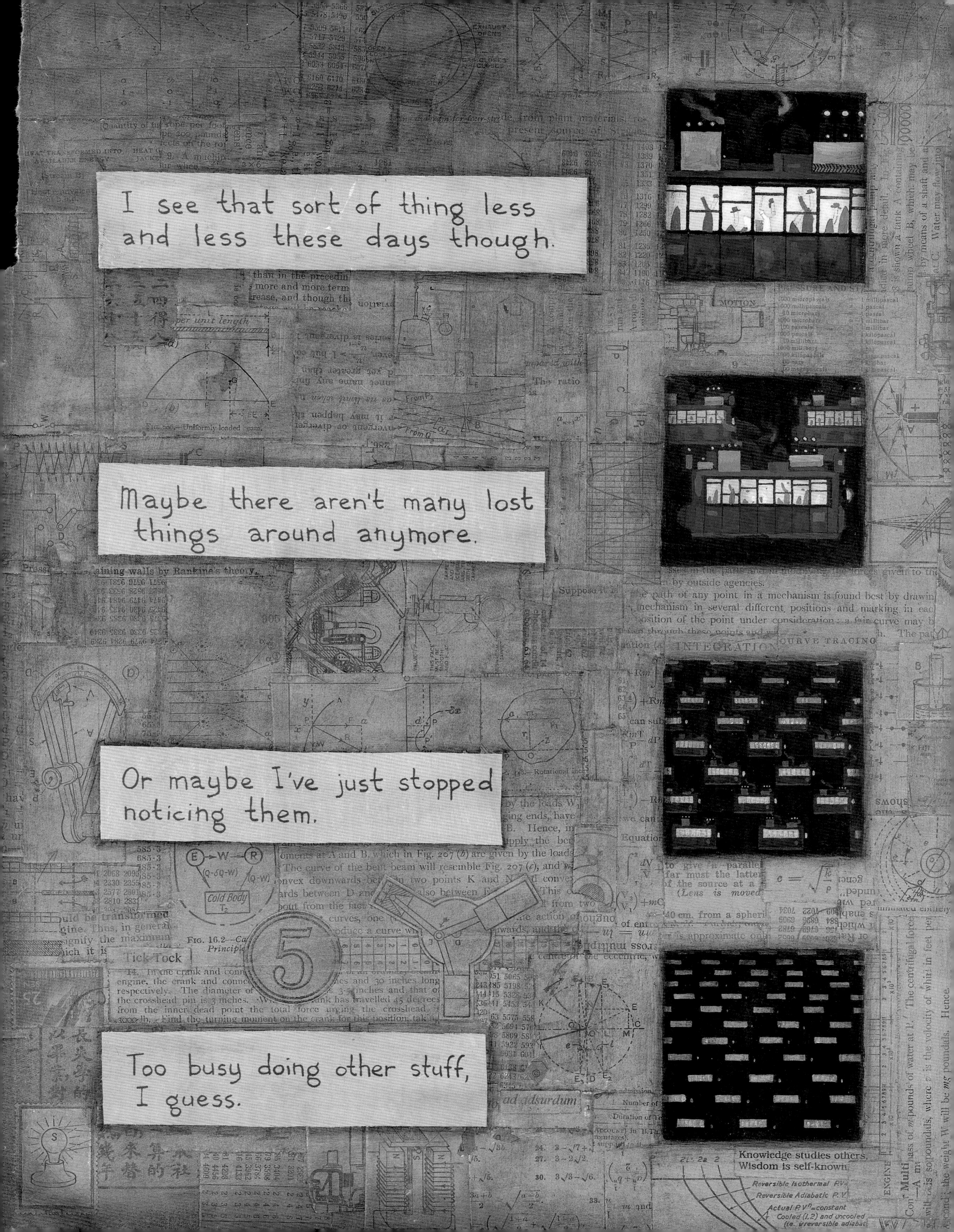
I see that sort of thing less and less these days though.
Maybe there aren't many lost things around anymore.
Or maybe I've just stopped noticing them.
Too busy doing other stuff, I guess.

And APOLOGIES to
Jeffrey Smart
Edward Hopper
& John Brack
and for valued interest and comments from
Jonathan, Keira, Robin,
the freo lit centre folk,
BILL DAY
Gary Crew
The Funkmeister
Paul & The Twins.
with THANKS to
Helen Chamberlin
Editorial technician #264
Chris D.
a fellow connoisseur of
heavy duty industrial plumbing

A. W. S.
K. S. S.
J. B. M.
500 Lb. per sq. inch
63. $\frac{x}{2x^2-4}$.
66. $\frac{x}{1-6x^2}$.
Dry Saturated
Fuel
EXHAUST
COMFORTABLE & RELAXED
OBJECTS WITHOUT NAMES?
If
PARAGON VALVE